Postman Pat® and the Hungry Goat

SIMON AND SCHUSTER

Postman Pat had a busy day ahead! Mrs Goggins had given him a pile of letters and three big parcels to deliver. There was a square package for PC Selby, a squashy one for the vicar, and a long flat one for Ajay. Pat struggled out of the Post Office and nearly collided with Dr Gilbertson.

Dr Gilbertson helped Pat get the parcels into his van. "Jess not with you today?" she asked.

"No, he's with Julian and Meera. They're putting up a tent in the garden."

"Ooh, camping. What fun!"

Pat's first stop was the Thompsons'. Alf was in the goat pen, feeding Rosie. "Hello there, Pat, come right in!"

As Pat went into the pen, Rosie made a dash for it. She jumped into Pat's van, and started chewing the labels off the parcels.

"Oh dear!" worried Pat, "I hope I can remember whose parcel is whose!"

"Sorry, Pat," sighed Dorothy. "That goat eats everything!"

"Rosie, you naughty thing, come 'ere!" cried Alf, but Rosie was off down the road in a flash. "Oh 'eck! There'll be no stoppin' her now!"

"We'll catch her up in the van," suggested Pat. "I'll deliver my parcels on the way."

Julian and Meera were having a bit of trouble of their own. The tent was harder to put up than they thought, and they ended up in a big tangle!

Luckily, Jess found the sheet of instructions in the tent bag.

"Well done, Jess!" grinned Julian. "Now we can put the tent up properly!"

Reverend Timms was watering his flowers when Pat and Alf drove up.

"Hello, vicar," called Pat, "I've got a parcel for you!"

"How lovely!" smiled Reverend Timms.

"I hope it's the right parcel. Alf's goat ate the labels!" explained Pat.

"Have you seen her, vicar?" asked Alf.

"No, I've been out here all morning, looking after my . . . oh dear!"

Rosie was munching away at the vicar's flowers.

"I'm right sorry, vicar," said Alf. "We'd better catch Rosie before she eats anything else, Pat."

"Too late, Alf," said Pat, as Rosie scampered off.

PC Selby
had just
finished
hanging
out his
washing.
He didn't
see Rosie
eyeing
up his
trousers . . .

But when Pat arrived, PC Selby was very cross.

"Hello, there, Arthur, delivery for you," said Pat. "And have you seen a goat, by any chance?"

"A goat, is it? Well, if I catch that goat, it's in a lot of trouble. It's eaten my best trousers!"

"Sorry, Arthur," said Alf, "can't stop – we've got to find Rosie!"

Pat gave PC Selby the long, thin package and zoomed off down the road.

"Oi! What about my trousers?" called PC Selby.

Pat and Alf delivered the last parcel to Ajay.

"Oh good," Ajay smiled. "I've been waiting for my new 'left luggage' sign. Hmm, this feels a bit squashy to me . . . Hey! My flowers!"

Rosie was having another little snack.

"Now's our chance, Pat," shouted Alf. But Rosie scarpered before they got close.

Pat and Alf searched all over Greendale, but Rosie was nowhere to be found.

"Ooh 'eck, Pat," sighed Alf. "Where can that goat be?"

"We'll just have to keep looking, Alf. We can't give up now!"

Julian and Meera hadn't given up either – the tent was finally up!

"Well done, you two," grinned Sara. "Now it's picnic time."

Julian and Meera laid the food out on a blanket but while they went to fetch the sausages and lemonade. . .

. . . the picnic vanished!

"Oh no!" wailed Julian. "Who's eaten our picnic?"

"Hmm, I've an idea who it might be," sighed Alf, as he and Pat walked over.

"We followed a trail of petals here," added Pat. "Now where is that pesky goat?"

At that very moment, Rosie popped her head out of the tent!

"Rosie!" scolded Alf.

ust then, the vicar, Ajay and PC Selby arrived, carrying their unwrapped parcels.

"My pyjamas!" smiled the vicar.

"My sign!" chuckled Ajay.

"My helmet!" muttered PC Selby, getting out his notebook.

"Sorry!" said Pat. "I must have got them muddled up when Rosie ate the labels."

"By gum, Rosie," gulped Alf. "We'd better get you back in your pen!"

"Let's take her in my van, Alf," offered Pat.

Julian and Meera laid a trail of sandwiches for Rosie and she munched them all the way into Pat's van.

"Right, Alf!" laughed Pat. "Last delivery of the day!"

They were pleased to get Rosie home.

"Thanks, Pat," said Alf.

"What a lot of trouble Rosie's caused!" said Dorothy.
"We must have a picnic for everyone to say sorry."

"Grand idea!" smiled Pat.

Dorothy made a lovely picnic. She gave the vicar a new pot of flowers. "Looks like I've got a pair of trousers to mend too!" she giggled.

"Mmm, delicious cake, Dorothy," said Reverend Timms. "Perhaps Rosie should get out more often!"

"I don't think Rosie will be getting out again in a hurry," chortled Pat. "She's got a special police guard."

PC Selby stood firm by Rosie's pen. Nobody noticed as she squeezed her head through the fence and took a bite out of his new helmet!

SIMON AND SCHUSTER
First published in 2005 in Great Britain by Simon & Schuster UK Ltd
Africa House, 64-78 Kingsway
London WC2B 6AH
A CBS COMPANY

This hardback edition published in 2007

Postman Pat® © 2005 Woodland Animations, a division of Entertainment Rights PLC
Licensed by Entertainment Rights PLC
Original writer John Cunliffe
From the original television design by Ivor Wood
Royal Mail and Post Office imagery is used by kind permission of Royal Mail Group plc
All rights reserved

Text by Alison Ritchie © 2005 Simon & Schuster UK Ltd

All rights reserved including the right of reproduction in whole or in part in any form

A CIP catalogue record for this book is available from the British Library upon request

ISBN-10: 1-84738-082-4
ISBN-13: 978-1-84738-082-1

Printed in China
1 3 5 7 9 10 8 6 4 2

To Jacqueline Korn, with
my love and my thanks ~ M.M.

To my big brothers, who saved me
from invaders from across the
cold North Sea in 1941 ~ M.F.

ACKNOWLEDGEMENTS

I am not a scholar of Old English literature,
so my research for this retelling was necessarily
gleaned from other retellings and translations
by poets and scholars and storytellers. Amongst
many sources of inspiration for my own telling
of *Beowulf* have been versions by the following
writers and poets: Seamus Heaney, Rosemary
Sutcliff, Kevin Crossley-Holland and
Michael Alexander. ~ M.M.

First published 2006 by Walker Books Ltd

87 Vauxhall Walk, London SE11 5HJ

This edition published 2007

2 4 6 8 10 9 7 5 3 1

Text © 2006 Michael Morpurgo   Illustrations © 2006 Michael Foreman

The right of Michael Morpurgo and Michael Foreman to be identified
as author and illustrator respectively of this work has been asserted by them
in accordance with the Copyright, Designs and Patents Act 1988

This book has been typeset in Poliphilus

Printed in China

British Library Cataloguing in Publication Data:
a catalogue record for this book is available from the British Library

ISBN 978-1-4063-0597-5

www.walkerbooks.co.uk

Beowulf

As told by *Michael Morpurgo*

Illustrated by *Michael Foreman*

WALKER BOOKS
AND SUBSIDIARIES
LONDON · BOSTON · SYDNEY · AUCKLAND

BEOWULF AND GRENDEL, THE MONSTER OF THE NIGHT

Hear, and listen well, my friends, and I will tell you a tale that has been told for a thousand years and more. It may be an old story, yet, as you will discover, it troubles and terrifies us now as much as ever it did our ancestors, for we still fear the evil that stalks out there in the darkness and beyond. We know that each of us in our time, in our own way, must confront our fears and grapple with this monster of the night who, given a chance, would invade our homes, and even our hearts, if he could.

So roll back the years now, back to the fifth century after the birth of Christ, and come with me over the sea to the Norse lands we now know as Sweden and Norway and Denmark, to the ancient

Viking lands of the Danes and the Geats, the Angles and the Jutes. This will be our here and now, as this tale of courage and cruelty unfolds, as brave Beowulf battles with the forces of darkness, first with that foul fiend Grendel, then with his sea-hag of a mother, and last of all, with the death-dragon of the deep.

The story begins as all stories do, before it begins, for there is always a mother before a mother, and a king before a king. In Denmark all the great lords, those royal descendants of Scyld, that great and good king, followed in his footsteps and stayed strong against their foes and loyal to their friends. The kingdom prospered. From their conquests the land grew rich, so that the people flourished and were happy. Feared by their enemies, loved by their allies, the kingdom of the Danes became great and powerful in the world.

Then the lord Hrothgar came to the throne, son of the old King Healfdene, great grandson of Scyld, and he was to become the greatest warrior king of them all. Fierce in battle, he fetched back home more treasures from his conquests than had ever before been seen or even dreamt of in Denmark. But he was generous too and a good father to his people, so that they obeyed him always gladly. Hearing of his increasing glory in battles, more and more warriors came to join him. It seemed to them and to him that there could never be an end to all his power and wealth. The kingdom was safe from its enemies, the people warm at their hearths and well fed. Truly it was a land of sweet content.

To celebrate these years of prosperity and plenty, Hrothgar decided he would raise for his people a huge mead-hall. It must, he declared, be larger and more splendid than any mead-hall ever built. Only the best timbers were used, only the finest craftsmen. At Hrothgar's bidding they came from all over Denmark to construct it, so that in no time at all the great hall was finished. It was truly even more magnificent than he had ever imagined it could be. Heorot he called it, and at the first banquet he gave there, Hrothgar, by way of thanks, gave out to each and every person rings and armbands of glowing gold. No king could have been kinder, no people as proud and as happy. Night after night they feasted in Heorot, and listened to the music of the harp and song of the poet. And every night the poet told them that story they most loved to hear: how God had made the earth in all its beauty, its mountains and meadows, seas and skies; how he had made the sun and the moon to light it, the corn and the trees to

grow on it; how he gave life and being to every living creature that crawls and creeps and moves on land or in the sea or in the air. And man too he made to live in this paradise. Around the warming hearth they listened to the poet's story, enraptured, enthralled and entranced.

But there was another listener. Outside the walls of Heorot in the dim and the dark there stalked an enemy from hell itself, the monster Grendel, sworn enemy of God and men alike, a beast born of evil and shame. He heard that wondrous story of God's good creation, and because it was good it was hateful to his ears. He heard the sweet music of the harp, and afterwards the joyous laughter echoing through the hall as the mead-horn was passed around. Nothing had ever so enraged this beast as night after night he had to listen to all this happiness and harmony. It was more than his evil heart could bear.

The night Grendel struck was the darkest night of all. He waited until Hrothgar had gone to his bed, until only the lords who nightly guarded Heorot were left. They were fast asleep when he pounced. He was upon them so suddenly and with such violence and fury that none could escape the terrible slaughter. Thirty lords he murdered in

his bloodlust, as savage and swift in his death-dealing as a maddened fox in a chicken hut. He left not one of them alive, but carried them off home to his lair to feast on their blooded corpses at his leisure. Only when day broke did Hrothgar and his warriors discover the dreadful evidence of the holocaust at Heorot. Gone now were the laughter and the music. Hrothgar sat silent in his grief and despair. His warriors too mourned and lamented the loss of their friends and brothers-in-arms. All were stunned at the merciless cruelty of this fatal fiend of the darkness. But the horrors were not yet over, for the next night Grendel came again, stalking over the foggy moors and down through the forests towards Heorot. The warriors had barricaded themselves in this time, and believed they must be safe. They could not have known that against this hellish monster all such defences would be useless. In a frenzy of hate, Grendel burst in and slaughtered everyone he found there, gorging himself at will. He spared no one.

From that night on, no one, not even Hrothgar, dared sleep again in Heorot. And so the great mead-hall stood empty, and stayed empty. Grendel the monster now ruled in Denmark, a rule of terror that haunted Hrothgar and all his people, wherever they lived, men, women and children alike. For twelve long winters Grendel warred unceasingly on the Danes, picking his blood victims at random, the innocent and the sick too, children and newborn babes. He was utterly without mercy.

Again and again he came to his killing ground, always unseen in the black of night. No plan Hrothgar and the council thanes devised could protect them from his fury, no prayers to the Almighty, no sacrifices to ancient heathen gods. Anywhere he struck, any farmstead, any cottage. Anywhere and everywhere. Nothing could put an end to these endless terror raids. A great and terrible grief darkened the land, banishing all happiness, all hope. Even the noble Hrothgar sat sunk in sorrow. Deep in his despair the Danish king could see no reprieve from this hideous nightmare visited so often upon his people by this fearful monster.

By now the story of this dreadful tragedy, of the nightly suffering Hrothgar and his people were enduring, had spread far and wide. They had heard about it too across the water in the land of King Hygelac of the Geats, for a long time faithful allies of the Danish kingdom. But only one of them, the greatest and bravest of all princes – Beowulf he was called – decided this evil beast of the night must be punished for all his wrongdoing, that Heorot must be cleansed of this wickedness and Hrothgar and his people saved at last, even if Beowulf had to give his own life to achieve it. Family and friends, Edgetheow his father, and his uncle the good King Hygelac himself, all of them did what they could to dissuade him from this reckless, perilous mission. But all advice, all omens, only whetted Beowulf's determination to go to Denmark and slay this monster of the night. He ordered a strong and seaworthy ship to be fitted out for the quest, and hand-picked fourteen of the fiercest warriors he knew. Out of the sheltered fjord they rowed this sturdy warship, and set sail for Denmark, riding the wind-whipped waves over the sea.

In brisk breezes the ship fair flew along, ploughing the storm-tossed ocean, until at last the shadow of land along the horizon became the rearing cliffs and capes of Denmark. Soon Beowulf and his ringmailed thanes were leaping ashore, each one thanking God most fervently for his safe arrival. From the cliff high above them Hrothgar's startled watchman saw men land, and wondered who they were, whether friend or foe. He rode down to the beach straight away and challenged them at the point of his spear. "Who are you, strangers? Where do you come from? I see you dressed and armed as warriors ready for battle. In all my years patrolling this coast no one has landed more openly. You do not come like thieves in the night, and your faces speak to me of some honest purpose. And I can plainly see that your prince, who stands head and shoulders higher than the rest of you, has the look of a hero about him, of great nobility and grace. Yet you are not known to us. Certainly Hrothgar has had no warning of your coming. So tell me your names and declare your intent frankly so I may know whether to let you pass or not."

Beowulf spoke up then, opening his heart honestly to the Danish coastguard. "We have come here from my lord Hygelac, king of the Geats, your ally and your good friend. All the world knows of the piteous misfortune that has befallen this land, of that marauding monster Grendel and all his murderous massacres. We have come here to destroy him if we can. So lead us to Hrothgar, that great and glorious guardian of his people.

Take us to Heorot, the heart of his kingdom, and take us there as fast as possible. There is no time to lose."

"You sound to me and you look to me like a man of your word," replied the coastguard. "So accepting all in good faith, I will bring you myself to Heorot, to my lord Hrothgar, who will, I know, rejoice at your coming. Meanwhile while you are gone on your great and noble quest, my men will see to it that your ship is well guarded."

So in war-dress of chainmail shirts, carrying their long ashen spears and great war-shields, Beowulf and his warriors left their ship anchored fast in the lee of the cliff, and marched inland, their helmets gleaming bright in the afternoon sun; strong helmets that would surely protect them against the worst any enemy could do, or so they thought. On they went until they saw at long last, in the distance, Hrothgar's home, Heorot, that glorious palace adorned with glowing gold, a house fit for any king on earth. Here the coastguard left them, pointing the way. "I must return to resume my watch for sea-raiders," he said. "May the God we all love protect you in all you do, wherever you go, and bring you safely back to your ship again, and back to your hearth and home."

Weary now from their long sea journey Beowulf and his war-band made their way up the stone path towards the great hall of Heorot, where they were greeted at the gate by Wulfgar, Hrothgar's herald. "Lay aside your shields and spears," he commanded them. "Stack them against the wall, for you will have no need of them inside. I see friendship in your eyes, nobility in your bearing, and know that we have nothing to fear from you. But tell me who you are, and what you've come for, dressed as you are for war."

"I am Beowulf, prince of the Geats, nephew of Hygelac the king, and if you would kindly allow us to speak face to face with Hrothgar, your gracious king, we will explain to him in full the purpose of

our sea-tossed journey to the land of the Danes." Wulfgar the herald was as wise in judgement as he was fierce in war, and let them at once into Heorot to meet Hrothgar, his beloved master, grey-haired now with sorrowing.

"These men, grim though they may look in their mail-armour, have come in peace, I am sure of it, my king," Wulfgar declared before the king and his thanes. "Chief among them, and the renowned prince of the Geats, is the noble Beowulf, nephew of Hygelac, your friend and ally of a lifetime. Such a trusty man can only have come to help us, I think."

Sudden hope warmed the old king's heart as he looked upon Beowulf standing there before him. "You will not remember me," he said, "I knew you once as a child, when I came to the land of the Geats. Ever since then the Geats have been my lifelong friends and allies. You are most heartily welcome to Heorot, for I know of you by hearsay also. Everyone here does. I heard tell that you possess the strength of at least thirty men in each hand. I am thinking, and I am hoping and I am praying, that you might have been sent here to us by God himself as our salvation, to stand against Grendel, that fiend of the night. Perhaps, Beowulf, it is only you that has the power to deal the monster the death-blow we long for, the end he so richly deserves."

Mighty in his ring-meshed mail and gloriously helmed in silver, Beowulf stood tall before Hrothgar and his thanes, every one of them praying too that this man would indeed prove to be their earthly redeemer, their strong avenger. They listened well as he spoke. "I have come, great king of the Danes," Beowulf began, "as Hygelac's hearth-kinsman, and in his name I am here to serve you as I have served him in many a battle. All the Geats have heard of your plight, of this evil Grendel who, after the shadows fall,

prowls this hall, making of it his nightly lair. From seafarers and travellers we have learned how each night this most splendid of mead-halls must be surrendered to Grendel, the night stalker, how he preys foully on your people, eating their flesh, drinking their blood. I am no poet, my lord king, nor a harp player. I am a fighter. I am known at home and wherever I go as a warrior prince, as an enemy of all evil. I have only last year dealt death to five giants who threatened our land, broken their necks with my bare hands. I did the same to dozens of sea-serpents who plagued our waters. If I could do that much, I thought, then I could go over the sea to you, great Hrothgar, and offer to rid you of Grendel, this vile and loathsome destroyer. Why, I thought, should I not face him in a trial of strength and destroy the destroyer? So I stand here in Heorot, your kingly hall and home, with my good companions, ready and willing to serve you. All of us are strong and steadfast in our determination to drive out this evil once and for all, to bring peace and joy again to your kingdom and to restore you at last to your rightful hearth. Be assured, I shall do all that is in my power to achieve this. It is my promise."

All their long-lingering sorrow was banished as Hrothgar and his thanes listened to Beowulf's brave words and, looking upon him, no one there doubted for one moment that Beowulf could achieve and would achieve all he promised. "I have heard," Beowulf went on, "that Grendel never carries a weapon, no war axe, no sword, on his murderous missions. Well then, neither will I. I seek no advantage. I need no advantage. I will carry no shield, nor wear any armour. I shall go up against this beast bareheaded, just as I fought the giants and sea-serpents. With my bare hands I shall grapple with this foul fiend and fight him to the death. Whichever of us dies must face the Lord of Judgement, as we all must when the time comes. I ask only that, should the worst befall me, send to Hygelac, my king, this battle-shirt of chainmail I now wear. There will, I fear, be nothing of us left to bury, should this flesh-eating monster prevail over us. In that case, from all I hear, he would carry off our bloody corpses to his unlovely larder and feast on us as he has on so many brave men before us. But God willing it will not turn out like that."

Hrothgar rose slowly to his feet. "You cannot imagine what joy you bring us in coming here to Heorot," he cried. "For me and for all of Denmark it is truly a blessed and timely arrival. You shall, I promise you, be well rewarded for your kindness, your concern for us and for your great courage. We have been for twelve long years a people in pain, with nothing but fear and hate in our hearts. Sadly my hall and hearth companions have been sorely dwindled in numbers by the ravages of this ruthless killer. So many have tried to stand against him. Their courage whetted by beer, each roared his defiance, boasting, ale cup in hand, that he would wait here in Heorot after nightfall and tear the evil one limb from limb when he came. But when morning came it was always the same gruesome story. Heorot had become a slaughterhouse yet again, the walls blood-spattered and the floors blood-soaked, and my dear brave kinsmen all gone as meat to the monster's lair. But none of these was as mighty a warrior as you, Beowulf. They had courage in full measure, but not the strength. You have both. So, bring your men, sit down, eat with us and drink with us. Tell us the stories of your great exploits, for just to hear them would fill our hearts with new hope and happiness."

Then a space was cleared at the banqueting table for Beowulf and his Geats, and the horn of sweet mead was passed around from Geat to Dane and Dane to Geat. That evening the poet stood and sang his words, and the harp played softly, and the lilting lute and laughter echoed once again through the rafters of Heorot.

There were, it was true, some envious looks cast at Beowulf and his Geatish warriors, and some envious words too. Amongst the Danish thanes a few did not care to be outshone in this manner and felt their honour threatened. Some challenged Beowulf openly, questioning his proud claim that he would succeed in this fight where they had not, especially, they said, if he faced up to Grendel unarmed as he had proposed he would. Stung at these insults Beowulf spoke up strongly in his own defence. "Do not worry yourselves on our account. We'll soon show this monster Grendel strength, courage and a firmness of purpose he has never met before. Just because you have failed, don't imagine for one moment we shall do the same. We are made of sterner stuff than you think. Mark my words, by daylight the reign of this terror-tyrant will be over. We have come to do this, and with God's help we shall achieve it."

The more Hrothgar heard, that kind and generous king, that great father-protector and shepherd of all the Danes, the more he hoped, and then believed, that Beowulf could better the beast that night. Doubts disappeared and all envy too, as the harp music rose to the rafters and laughter echoed once again about the great mead-hall. Bearing the precious treasure-cup, Hrothgar's queen came now to Heorot to meet these Geatish heroes, to greet and honour them. But to the peerless Hrothgar, her husband and her beloved, she offered the treasure-cup first, and afterwards gave the cup to each of them, irrespective of age or rank, for she was always gracious and kind to all. Then to Beowulf she came, glittering in her regal beauty, her arm-rings glowing gloriously. Offering him the cup, she thanked him warmly, and the good Lord who had sent him, for coming so nobly to their aid.

Accepting the treasure-cup and her thanks most graciously, Beowulf rose to speak. "We have come here, my lady, rowed and sailed our way across the surging seas for only one reason, to carry out the wishes of great Hrothgar, your husband and king, and our friend and perfect ally; to accomplish the death of this Grendel and end for ever the terror that stalks this place and all your people, or to fail in the attempt and so meet our end."

No words had ever sounded sweeter to this lady, this splendid queen of the Danes. The poet sang then of the victory to come, of the foul fiend destroyed and evil banished, and Geat and Dane alike raised their rousing voices till all Heorot resounded once more to the ringing rafters. But now, as he looked out, Hrothgar saw the shadows lengthening and knew the time was coming to quit the hall. He knew, as they all did, that outside in the falling dark which would very soon drown the world, the dreaded monster was leaving his lair again, was already gliding through the brooding shadows towards Heorot.

Hrothgar and Beowulf, great heroes both, saluted one another in love; and, in parting, Hrothgar spoke his last words. "I now hand over

Heorot to you, brave Beowulf, to have and to hold through this night. Guard it well. I know that in the fight to come you will stretch every sinew, summon up all the strength and all the courage you possess. In return, should you survive and the beast be destroyed, I promise before everyone here, I will show you more generosity than a king ever showed before to any man." So saying, Hrothgar and his queen led the Danes from the hall. Only Beowulf and his Geatish thanes remained, charged now with the safety of the kingdom. "The time is soon coming. So let each of us put our trust in God," said Beowulf to his men, "but in our strength and fighting skills also. Do this and we shall not fail." And with that he took off his coat of mail and his helmet, as he had vowed to do. He unbuckled his war-sword too, and then gave all his armour and weapons to his faithful attendant.

Before going to their beds the Geats gathered together one last time, set forehead to forehead, drinking deep of one another's courage, fiercer now than ever in their fiery determination. "We ask the Lord to bless our endeavours tonight," Beowulf whispered. "Remember we fight this fight in his name. It would be easy to come at the beast with weapons. But I shall cut short this monster's life with my own God-given strength. Let God choose which of us shall triumph and we have no fear of losing. Believe that, my friends, and we shall win."

So Beowulf went to his bed, and his men too, but in truth they slept only fitfully, for there was not one of them, not Beowulf himself even, who could be certain how the night would end, whether any of them would ever again see the light of dawn. They knew well enough how many brave Danes this Grendel creature had dragged lifeless and bleeding from Heorot, how unlikely it was that some, or all of them, would ever again see their hearth and home. In silent prayer, each of them placed his life in the hands of his Almighty Maker who had from the very beginning ruled supreme in all the affairs of men.

Up from his lair and through the shadows came Grendel, this stalker of the night, while in Heorot the warriors lay turn-tossed in their sleep, only one of them left on ever watchful guard, every moment steeling himself for the ordeal of battle he knew must very soon

come. And it was coming too. Grendel came gliding through swirling moorland cloud-mists, death-dealing in his hate-filled heart, thirsting to kill again that night as he had so often before. Down from the forest came Grendel now, saw the mead-house, scented the sweet flesh of those inside, easy victims; as easy as before, he thought.

Had the monster known what awaited him there, he would most surely have thought twice, slunk back to his lair and never returned, for this would be the last time the beast was ever to go out on a killing spree. Never more would the terror-tyrant stalk the land. Now it was his turn to suffer the panic of fear, and the pain of death agony. So the giver of death and destruction would become the receiver at last. He did not know it yet though, and came on unawares to Heorot.

Rage-wracked, on wreckage bent, Grendel ripped open the iron-studded doors – they were no hindrance to him. He scanned the dark hall through fire-blazing eyes, saw the slumbering thanes, still drowsy in sleep, the solitary, startled sentry, the whole war-band. Rejoicing at the prospect of another flesh-feast, this vile and vengeful creature laughed out loud at his good fortune. He would tear each and every one of them to pieces, stain Heorot's floor once more with the lifeblood. A night of gore and gluttonous pleasure lay ahead of him, or so it seemed. And so it began, too, as he snatched up the first Geatish sentry he saw, Handscio he was called, and simply tore him apart, bolting his flesh in great gobbets, gnawing and gnashing on his bones, stripping the meat, sucking the veins, until, in moments, nothing of the poor helpless man was left, not a hair of his head, not a hand, not a foot, not even a nail.

That was just the beginning for him, he thought. Onto his next victim he pounced at once, reaching out to grab him with his killing claws. But now he was met with a grip of steel, a grip harder, tighter, than he had ever known, that seized him, held him fast by the arm. Locked in the vice of this grip he could not break free, however much he struggled, and he knew at once he had met his match. Filled with sudden fear the monster struggled again and again to unloose this fist, yearning only now to be away from Heorot and home again in the safety of his lair. Vainly he tried to pull away, but Beowulf's fingers fastened harder still in an ever tightening grip around that callous killer's arm.

How Grendel longed to get out, to escape to the forests and fens, but no power on this earth could force Beowulf to release his grip. Now Grendel knew, this merciless, murderous ogre, that he should never have come this night, that his death was coming and that, despite all his efforts to tear himself away, there was nothing he could do to prevent it, no way he could save himself. Fear of this death drove him mad with anger, and anger only made him stronger; he would fight to the death to save himself. He would never give in.

It was amazing that the great hall of Heorot was not split asunder that night, so ferocious was the wrestling between these two giants. Locked together in this deadly embrace they reeled and writhed about the mead-hall, so that all the Danes outside could hear a dreadful cacophony of crashing and crying resounding through Heorot. Gold-worked trappings and iron braces, all well made and sturdy, simply snapped and buckled as the two of them in deadly earnest wrestled and grappled and struggled with one another. There was no ground given in this terrible fight, nor mercy either. So they fought on, this Grendel now fear-soaked, his strength failing him, and brave Beowulf, fist still clenched around the monster's arm and knowing he had only to cling on and not let go to banish to hell for ever the damned one, God's and his own worst enemy. Clearly outside they heard the monster's demon scream, his hideous, howling screech. The sound of it chilled every listener to the bone, yet hope gladdened them too, for these they knew were not human cries, but rather the strident sobbing of the beast in agony and terror.

Seeing Grendel thus pinioned by the Geatish hero, and tortured and weakened by his pain, Beowulf's companions-in-arms drew their swords and sprang now to his side to help him in his fight, to finish if they could this murderer's wretched life. They were not to know, Beowulf's battle-friends, that no man-made sword, no steel could pierce this cruel creature's enchanted hide. Only naked strength could end his unnatural life. Grendel understood this, and he knew he was weakening, that his end must be near. He could think of no possible way to escape. Great-hearted Beowulf, sensing his sagging strength, had him still by the arm, now twisted it and turned it until the shoulder muscles split apart, the tendons snapped, the bone joints burst, and Grendel's arm was ripped and wrenched, bleeding, from his body.

Then Grendel fled armless and half dead already from Heorot. Over the moors he staggered and stumbled, through the fens back to his den, knowing all the while that this was his last day on earth, that his life's blood was draining from him. He was dying his death.

So Beowulf the Good had triumphed in his bitter fight with Grendel the evil one. Thus were all Danish hopes fulfilled and Beowulf's promise to them too. He had destroyed the great destroyer with his bare hands, saved Hrothgar's royal mead-house and the Danish people from further terrors, and given them back the sanctuary of their hearth, and their home. So that everyone should know that the tyrant was truly dead and their grief finally at an end, the hero hung high in the gables of Heorot, where all could see it and marvel at it too, that whole torn-off limb, shoulder, arm and hand, gruesome witness to the monster's violent end.

By the next morning the news of the great fight at Heorot had spread throughout the land. They came in their hundreds from the seashore, from the fens and moors and mountains, from near and far to see this hideous limb hanging there in the hall, and then to follow the fiendish foe's last footprints through the shadowy forest and the moor-mist, tracking the trail of blood to the monster's marsh-pool. To this remote and dismal place the dying monster had come only hours before, the last of his blood ebbing fast with every faltering step. Here he had dived to his miserable death, his hot wound-blood bubbling and boiling in the brackish waves. So he had sunk at last to his cavernous lair below, and had died there alone in his agony, to be welcomed back in hell where he belonged.

Beowulf's marvellous feat was now the talk of Heorot and all the Danish lands beyond. None was his equal, they said, none braver, nor more worthy, even, to be king here in Denmark in his own right. And this was not said to slight great Hrothgar, for he was a good and much loved king of his people, but only in praise of Beowulf and his great courage and strength. That day the poet wove his word-song, told the story of the hero in glowing, golden language, rang the word-changes, and all who were there remembered and told it again and again, so that their children and their children's children should never forget his daring deeds, nor the noble name of Beowulf either.

That evening all were summoned to Heorot, to that splendid mead-hall freed now for ever from Grendels's evil reign and cleansed of the night's horrors. Beowulf the Great, as guest of honour, came in with Hrothgar the king, and his glorious queen, with all her maidens following. And gathering there now too, thronging Hrothgar's happy hall, were all the thanes and warriors, anyone who could find a place, each of them gazing in awe at the sight of Grendel's dreadful arm hanging there from the rafters. But it was not chiefly this grisly reminder they had come for, but to see Beowulf, their great champion, sitting beside good King Hrothgar, and to show their joyous triumph and their relief at this timely and blessed deliverance.

Taking his stand on the steps, his queen and Beowulf on either side, Hrothgar began his speech of thanks and all there listened to every gracious word. "Let our thanks be first to God above for his mercy. To the Master of Heaven and master of this earth, worker of all miracles, for it is he who has brought Grendel to his death at last. I will be honest with you. Until yesterday, until Beowulf came, I doubted whether Grendel – and I curse his name for all the grief he brought to us – could ever be overcome, whether this loveliest of mead-halls could ever be truly ours again, whether the damned demon's bloodletting slaughter could ever be brought to an end. Then God sent us this man, this hero amongst men, now here at my side, the noble Beowulf, and his companions-in-arms; and together they have achieved in one night what we had tried and failed to do in twelve long years of sorrow. What mother would not have been proud to have borne such a son as this? What father does not yearn for a son like Beowulf? So Beowulf, best of men, from this moment I cherish you as I would my own son. And as I promised before, anything that is in my gift you shall have – it will be small reward for your great service to us all. Know also that your deeds will bring you greater riches still, which are my undying honour and gratitude and love, and that of all my people too. May Almighty God grant you always the success you enjoyed last night wherever you go, whatever the fight, whoever the foe may be." And the cheering that followed this rang loud in the rafters of Heorot, and was only silenced when Beowulf himself began to speak. It was not at all in a proud or boasting tone – that was never his way.

"We came here willingly, my warriors and I, to challenge the evil one on your behalf, and with God's help we prevailed. Yet I am sorry you see hanging up there only his arm. I should have preferred you to have seen the rest of him here too. I tried my utmost to hold him fast, to squeeze the life out of him, but I did not have a good enough grip of him to prevent his escape. By

tearing himself away and leaving behind his arm, he must have hoped to save himself from death, wretched creature. But God did not wish it, and so the fiend lives no more. He will no more haunt your land or plague your people. Like any other murderous criminal he awaits now God's own justice. We may have his arm, but God has his evil soul and will do with him as he pleases."

All the talk was then of the fine words they had just heard, and of what a furious fight it must have been during that perilous night when Beowulf destroyed the beast. Long they gazed at the grotesque arm up there, at the horrible hand and fearsome fingers, the nails as strong and sharp as steel, each one a spur-talon, each a vicious war-weapon for gouging and gashing. They shuddered to look at it, to think what damage it could do, and marvelled once again at Beowulf's bravery.

Then Hrothgar the king ordered the banqueting hall to be made ready at once for a feast. How willingly they went to work to prepare the place, adorning it richly from golden gable to shining floor. They hung glowing, gold-wrought tapestries. They mended or covered all the damage and destruction that greatest of all mead-halls had suffered the night before, and prepared a great feast of thanksgiving, as the king had commanded.

That evening when all was ready, into that happy hall came Hrothgar and Beowulf again. All around them now, on the mead-benches, sat the thanes and warriors and as many of the good people of Denmark as the benches would allow. Hrothgar's queen was there of course, all her ladies, and all the Geatish warriors too. And all rejoiced and feasted as never before, the mead-cup passing from hand to hand, until Heorot was filled once more with the laughter of friends, with sweet song and marvellous music, with unbounded joy.

Then offering him the cup the queen spoke to Hrothgar. "Now my lord and king, to these Geats speak graciously and generously, and let your gift-promise not be forgotten now, for Heorot is ours again, cleansed of evil and bright again with joy." To Beowulf next she came with the cup, where he sat between her two sons, Hrethric and Hrothmund. And when he had drunk, then came the time of gifts. Two arm-wreaths were brought, and robes and more gold rings; but best of all – the richest collar, the finest prize; more ornate and finely wrought than any I ever saw, the most treasured jewel Hrothgar possessed, worn on the neck of great war-kings and heroes; a fabled collar for an already fabled warrior. "It is no more than you deserve, Beowulf," said Hrothgar's fair queen, and all listened when she spoke and agreed wholeheartedly. "May good fortune come with these jewels, and may the rest of your life be always filled with happiness and prosperity. And may treasure come your way often and in large amounts! Be strong but be gentle too, and a wise guardian too to my two boys. By them, and by me and my lord Hrothgar, your name will be held in honour and love till the end of time."

How they cheered the queen's words then, those thanes and lords and ladies, and what a sumptuous feast it was of wine and food, and all held in a perfect harmony of joy and hope. They did not know then that the joy would be short-lived, the hope destroyed before even the night was over.

BEOWULF AND THE SEA-HAG

As the night shadows fell over Heorot, Hrothgar and his queen escorted Beowulf and all the Geatish heroes to their beds, leaving the great mead-hall in the care of the thanes of Denmark. They cleared away the benches and spread the floor with beds and bolsters and, as so often they had done before, made a dormitory of the great hall. Out of habit these warriors kept their weapons near to hand, always ready for war, their shields and hand-swords at their sides, and, on the benches nearby, their mail-coats, their mighty helmets and spears. But not one of them expected any attack that night. Safe in their hall, so they thought, they fell asleep at once and slept soundly. It was a sleep they would pay for dearly and soon.

For Grendel had a mother, a murderous hag, as hideous a monster as her fiend of a son. Now she was a bereaved mother out for revenge, maddened by her loss, and she would be savage in her grief. With vengeance brimming in her soul she came to Heorot in the dead of that night, all the Danish lords fast asleep inside, each lost in his dreams. How quickly were these dreams turned into a sudden nightmare! She may not have had the monster strength of her son, but she was thirsting for blood as she came in amongst them and powerful in her fury. The thanes quickly roused themselves from their slumbers, sprang at once to arms to fight her off, but they were not quick enough. She tore down Grendel's arm, that hideous trophy, but so precious to her.

 She snatched up the sleeping Ashhere, Hrothgar's most favourite lord, and then, seeing so many swords raised against her, made her escape. She had to be satisfied with this one kill. It was revenge enough for her. Away over the high moors she went in the darkness, clutching in her fierce embrace the bleeding Ashhere, found her way back to her distant fen to gorge herself on his flesh. How sweet was the taste of vengeance to this horrible hag.

Meanwhile all Heorot was in uproar. Swiftly summoned to the hall Hrothgar heard the dreaded news that Ashhere was dead and gone, his beloved friend murdered. He called at once for Beowulf. Who else would he turn to? Ashhere could not be saved, not now. Not even Beowulf, that victory-blest Geat could do that, but if anyone could destroy this demon-mother it was him. The wise old king, distraught with sadness, opened his word-hoard, and spoke his heart to the Geatish prince. "Ashhere was my hearth-companion, my best and oldest friend. Side by side we stood in many a bloody battle, striking for our lives, for each other. And now he's dead, no more than a meal-feast for Grendel's blood-lusting mother. Last night for us you killed her son, tore the life out of him, and now she has had her grim revenge. I do not know and I cannot tell where she is gone to, but country people have often told stories of two such ogres haunting the high moors and mists. One of them it was said was more woman in shape than man, a twisted monster-woman,

they said, a giant of a creature, demonic and unnatural. The othe[r]
they called Grendel, that fiend from hell you so bravely des[troyed].
We thought at first these were mere imaginings. Sto[ries of]
simple people with simple minds. How wron[g we were, and how]
bitterly we have paid for it. They never [saw this other]
monster – though all of them said [it was far bigger than Grendel]
himself. But time and again [they had seen it moving in the]
moor-mists.

"None of them ever dared venture [to the dark lake wh]ere the
monster and his mother lived, for it [is said to b]e a place of
wolves, of wild moors, dark fells and [perilo]us paths. Somewhere
there, they said, a torrent of water plunges into the deep earth to
make an underground channel that passes through vaulting
caverns. Here these ogres had their loathsome lair. It is no
distance from here, but no man of sense has ever ventured near
the place. Even a wounded stag, hard pressed by baying hounds
hot on his scent would rather face the hounds' tearing teeth than
plunge into that bottomless stream. Sometimes I have heard that
these waters stir themselves into such a rage that they swirl up
into the clouds and the whole earth weeps in terror.

"I have no one else to turn to. If you dare, as you dared before, then
find this hideous sea-hag, seek her out in her unlovely lair and
destroy her. I shall reward you as I did before, with golden
treasures from my hoard. My generosity will be even greater this
time, I assure you."

Then Beowulf, Edgetheow's noble son replied. "For a fighting man like me, daring is everything. How else will a fighting man be remembered if he does not dare? I cannot banish your grief, great king. But I can and will avenge your loss. Of that you can be sure. I shall quickly find where this hag of hell has gone to. And I promise there will be nowhere she can hide, no fold in the field, no ditch, forest or craggy cleft, no watery haven, nowhere. However deep she dives, I shall find her, and when I do your revenge and mine will be swift and sure."

So they rode out after her together, Danish king and Geatish hero, their lords and thanes beside them, their shieldbearers marching alongside. It was not difficult to see which way she had gone. Along woodland paths, over the high moors foul with fog they traced her bloody steps, following where she had

gone before, dragging her bloody victim. The trail narrowed between the cliffs and the path here was tortuous and treacherous. Up over the scree they went then and down again onto the fens, a haunted, dreadful place where no one could ever live, nor would ever wish to live.

Sensing danger all about them now Beowulf and his warriors went ahead to scout the land. They came then to a cheerless cluster of ash trees by a rushing stream that tumbled beneath a rocky crag, and beyond that they found a dark, deep lake, stained with blood. And all knew at once whose blood it was. Worse evidence was to come, for they saw left there on the edge of the cliff the most grievous sight, Ashhere's head. Stirred to new fury they let out an eager battle cry, sounded the war-horn loud and long so that the whole world could hear their anger.

Roused and enraged by the challenge of the battle-horn a giant sea-serpent slithered to the surface. They saw now that the lake was teeming with them, and with countless strangely writhing water-snakes too. This place was truly a home of monsters. Beowulf at once let loose an arrow, the iron tip striking home to its mark, deep in the sea-serpent's throat. Other spears then rained down until the body of this wave-lurker was dragged lifeless to the shore. Grisly, grim and gruesome – no one word could describe this ghoul of the deep. Everyone there was happy to see he was dead, I can tell you. But others were there, skulking shadows of the deep, waiting for Beowulf, waiting for their moment to strike.

Beowulf now made himself ready for the fight that lay ahead of him, putting on first his heavily mailed shirt, so strong that no enemy could pierce it. On his head he set a splendid silver helmet that would protect him, and ward off the worst of the blows. Wonderfully crafted it was, adorned with gold, richly carved all around with wild boars at bay — no sword-swipe had ever breached its stern defence. Unferth, Hrothgar's herald and counsellor, then handed him a hilted sword — Hrunting, he called it — a sword unlike any other, ancient, tried and tested, wave-patterned, iron-edged, imbued over the years with the blood and venom of those it had destroyed. This sword had never failed any hero before. Beowulf clutched it keenly, eager now to face the foe.

But first he spoke to silver-haired Hrothgar close beside him. "The time has come, great king, to test again my courage and my strength. Remember, wise lord, all that we agreed before the fight with Grendel, that should I die in your service, you will be like a father to me when I am gone, protecting my hearth-companions, and sending what gifts you have granted me, kind Hrothgar, to my lord Hygelac for his safe-keeping. Being his servant you will understand that all I have is his. It will show him how generous you have been, how you keep your word, and he will love you for it. And let Unferth have back Hrunting, the blade he just gave me. It should rightly be his again. With Hrunting I shall kill the ogress or die in the attempt. Let God choose between us."

With these words Beowulf, that daring prince, dived into the lake and disappeared. So deep was the perilous pool that it seemed to take for ever before he saw the bottom and felt it with his feet. And there that blood-greedy hag of the deep was waiting for him. Ready in ambush she sprang on him, fastening him at once with her hellish hooks. But although he was caught, Beowulf was so far unharmed, for her clenched claws could not pierce the mail-shirt and draw blood.

Pinioned and helpless in her grasp, the sea-hag dragged the prince to her cavernous lair. Try as he did Beowulf could not even draw his sword to defend himself against this water-wolf, nor against the onslaught of twisting sea-monsters now slashing at him with their tearing tusks that threatened to rip away his life-saving battle-coat. Still held fast in her deadly embrace Beowulf found himself hauled to the surface in a vaulted cavern lit all about with fires of hell it seemed, but at least he could breathe again, and was free of the pressing weight of water. At least now he would not simply be swept away and drowned. Then he looked up and saw the monstrous size of this hideous sea-hag — he had felt her strength already. Undaunted, he saw his chance. He broke free of her, tore himself away, drew Hrunting, circled it high above him and brought it screaming down on her head, sure it must be her death stroke. But Hrunting, that battle-hardened, all powerful sword that had sliced so easily through helmet and mail, could not bite this monster's hoary hide, but simply bounced off, leaving her flesh unharmed, unscathed, unmarked even. Never before had Hrunting failed a warrior in a fight as it had now.

But Beowulf, intent on victory, was not in the least downhearted. Rather his courage was renewed, his ferocity sharpened. Seeing its blade-edge would be useless, the hero flung Hrunting aside and trusted now, as he had before, to his own strength, to the God-given power in his hands. Now was not the moment to think of saving his life. Now would be his time of testing, his achieving of everlasting glory.

Anger steeled his strength, fury fired his determination, stirred him to action. Beowulf hurled himself at Grendel's mother, grabbed her by the shoulder and threw her bodily to the ground. But in a moment she repaid him fully, grasping him with her horrible hand-hooks, so that he stumbled and fell, too weary now to save himself. At once she was astride him. He was at her mercy. She snatched up her dagger. Now she would avenge her boy, her only son. With a scream of triumph she struck, but the mail-shirt shielded him from the sharp-edged blade, from the deadly point. Again and again she stabbed and slashed, but Beowulf's blessed battle-shirt did not fail him. Without it the Geat hero would certainly have been slaughtered there and then. But God, looking down, saved him, gave him the victory.

Summoning the last of his strength, Beowulf threw her off and leapt to his feet, and there above him on the wall he saw hanging an ancient war-trophy, a giant sword, so huge, so heavy that only a giant could wield it in battle-play. But this death-defying champion, this Geatish hero, was boiling with war-fury. Like this, he was as strong as any giant, and he knew it. He sprung to the wall, caught up the sword by its hilt, and whirling it once above his head, the blade singing out its death-song, he brought it down on her neck, in one blow cutting clear through bone and flesh. Her death-agony was swift, and when it was done she lay at his feet stilled by death, Beowulf's giant sword hot with her fiendish blood. It was over, it was done. The monster-mother was united in death at last with her monster son.

Looking about him now in that hell-hole, Beowulf saw scattered there the wretched remains of Hrothgar's brave hearth-companions, those that Grendel had murdered as they slept in Heorot hall. He saw too where Grendel himself lay, stiff in death, his lifeblood long ago drained from him. There was one more task for this giant sword. Beowulf, the fiercest of champions, finished the task and severed Grendel's hideous head with a single swipe.

Way up above, in the light of day, Hrothgar and his thanes, hearts heavy with anxiety, watched and waited by the pool. Fearful too were the Geatish warriors for their prince, especially when they saw blood bubbling up from the depths, marbling the surface of the water. Many long hours had passed now since Beowulf dived down into the deep, and most now believed that the famous hero could not this time be triumphant, but that the she-wolf, that devilish sea-hag, had at last done him to death.

As dusk came down over that dreary place, Hrothgar and his thanes turned sadly for home and hearth, all hope now abandoned. But the Geats stayed, stunned with grief, hoping against hope to see once more their beloved leader; but they knew well enough now that they would not.

Down below in the ogres' lair Beowulf looked about him in wonder at the heaped hoard of treasures, blood-booty of that damned pair. Much good it was to them now. The Geat hero took none of these treasures when he left, only the head of Grendel; Hrunting, the sword that had failed him; and the hilt of the giant sword that had done the she-wolf to death. Only the hilt remained of this deadly war-weapon – the engraved blade itself had simply been melted away by the hot blood of the doomed fiend that lay headless there.

So Beowulf, that sainted survivor, plunged once more into the deep and with powerful strokes swam upwards through the water, unhindered now by sea-serpents and writhing monsters of the deep, for the pool was now cleansed of these vile creatures, gone where all evil goes, where Grendel and his mother had gone, down to hell itself where they belonged, never to return again.

The first his faithful companions saw of their beloved prince was his silver war-helmet breaking the waves. Then, with spirits high with joy, they rushed to the water's edge to help him, wondering at his battle trophies, all of them thanking God for his victory and his safe return unharmed to their side. Quickly they loosened his mail-shirt and helmet, and all welcomed him joyously, good friends and loyal hearth-companions. So they left that dreadful pool behind them, blood-red from shore to shore, and still as death. It was a place all of them were happy to leave, Beowulf most of all.

A bold spring in their step, carefree now at heart, they followed the well-trodden path back towards Heorot. It was a triumphant procession, but a slow one, for that heavy head, Grendel's hideous head, had to be carried, and it was no easy matter I can assure you. It took four of the strongest Geats to hold the spear steady, the dreaded head stuck high on the point, glaring in death all about it as they went.

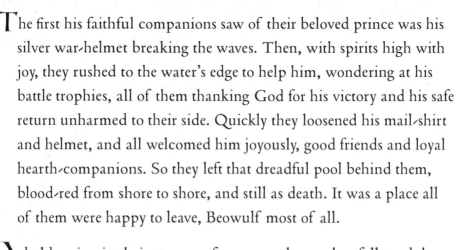

So with Grendel's head aloft they made their way to Heorot, fourteen brave Geats, and the great warrior prince. Marching into that splendid mead-hall they came, much to the surprise and joy of everyone there. As Beowulf held up that monstrous head by its unlovely locks, it was indeed as ugly a thing as any there had seen, an awesome sight, but one that no longer brought fear to their hearts, only rapturous relief and great gratitude towards this prince of warriors. They listened to him now, Hrothgar and his queen, and all the gathered thanes.

"We have brought back for you, great king of Denmark, all these trophies of our victory. They were heavy indeed to carry but our heart-song made light of the burden. I will not pretend to you it was easy, my lord. It was a close-run thing this fight under water, a fight I very nearly lost before it had begun. Hrunting, fine weapon though it is, was useless against this she-wolf of the deep. But God was with me, and I thank only him for my victory. I snatched up another

sword, a giant of a weapon, hanging there on the wall, and with it I avenged all the murder and misery inflicted on you by this family of fiends. First the monster's head I severed, then this grisly reminder still lying there from that earlier conflict. Your enemies are dead. You have your peace back, so all of you may now sleep safely in Heorot. We have seen the last of them, my lord king. Everyone here can rest assured of that, I promise you."

Then Beowulf presented to the silver-haired king the golden hilt, all that remained of the giant sword that had done such damage in the fight. So the hilt belonged fittingly to Hrothgar, the best and wisest of kings. He spoke now to the silent hall.

"Beowulf, my friend and best of men, your name and your nobility will resound throughout the world, even in the farthest corners. I marvel not only at your strength, but at the wisdom of one so young. Stay as generous and peaceable as you are, Beowulf. Do not become as other heroes have before you, so tuned to battle that a thirst for blood consumes you. I tell you this because I am old in years, and I know that all men, however noble and fine, are frail, and our lives are finite. At the height of our powers, when triumph succeeds triumph, we cannot imagine an end to our success. Pride grows within us, despite ourselves. We can easily forget that our powers are God-given, and should be used only in his service. Know, beloved Beowulf, that even with you the end must come, flesh and strength will fail. You are now in the high noon of your strength, but waiting for you, and not so far away, is sickness maybe, or a slashing sword, burning fire or drowning wave, the stab of a dagger, or just old age. Death awaits us all. I thank God in his great mercy my own death has been postponed long enough for me to enjoy this moment, the end of Grendel and his kind, to gaze in triumph at his gory head. So, remembering all this, let us all rejoice and feast together tonight. And in the morning I shall give you all your promised treasure."

But they did not feast long that night, for Hrothgar the old king was tired and wished to rest. No feast can continue without its host, and the truth was that the Geatish prince was ready for his bed too. He had earned his rest that night, I think. Battle-weary, the hero and his thanes slept deeply until the black raven in the tree outside raucously greeted the coming of the new day. Sunlight chased away the shadows as the prince and his companions made ready to leave. Now the fight was done they wanted to be home, every warrior among them. They had been away long enough. Before he left, Beowulf returned Hrunting to Unferth, the king's herald, and thanked him for the loan of it, without ever finding fault with the blade that had failed him. Beowulf was like this, fierce in battle, but generous and thoughtful in spirit. He did not want to hurt Unferth's feelings.

Now dressed in their armour and prepared for the journey home, Beowulf and his warriors went to Hrothgar to say their last farewells. The Geatish hero spoke first. "You will understand, great Hrothgar, how we long to return to Hygelac, to see once again our home and hearth. You have looked after us royally. We shall not forget your kindness. Know also, lord Hrothgar, that I shall always be ready to come to your aid again if you should ever need me. If I hear you are threatened by your neighbours, or that any intend you harm, I shall come back with a thousand warriors to help you. Hygelac, my young king, lord of the Geats, would, I know, always want me to be at your side, shoulder to shoulder, and defending you against your enemies, along with a forest of sharpened Geatish spears, if ever you should need us."

Saddened at this parting Hrothgar, wise in his great age, spoke to Beowulf, knowing that it was unlikely he would ever set eyes on his dear friend again. Tears filled his eyes as he embraced the Geatish hero for the last time. He spoke to him as a father to his favourite son. "I have never known a man at the same time so young and so wise. In you strength and wisdom are perfectly matched. How the Lord in Heaven has blessed you. If any ask me I shall say this:

should, God forbid, the Geats lose their renowned king through sword or sickness, they could not want for a better prince than you to take his place and rule over the kingdom. In coming here to help us you have brought our two peoples close together. By your courage you have banished any lingering ancient rivalries between Dane and Geat. So long as I am king, our ships will cross the seas between us filled not with spears, but only with gifts of friendship and love. We shall from now on stand always fast together, Sea-Geats and Spear-Danes, firm against our enemies."

So Beowulf left, carrying with him twelve new treasures, those promised parting gifts from the king to the Geatish hero, that dear man, friend for ever of the Danish king and his people. Gold-decked and resplendent with rings he left them, and not a Dane who watched him go believed the reward was any more than he deserved.

Now they came again to the sea-shore, sorrowing in their loss of Handscio, their dead war-companion, and at the same time rejoicing in all that had been achieved, and also in Hrothgar's generosity towards them. The coastguard who had greeted them days before saw them coming again, these young warrior heroes in their war-shirts and glittering helmets. He rode to greet them, guiding them to the waiting sea-boat he had guarded so carefully for them. Once the ship was loaded with horses and armour, and Hrothgar's hoard of gifts, Beowulf gave the coastguard a gift — a gold-hilted sword. It was a gift I am sure the man treasured for ever. Then a mist rose high over the deck, the slack sail hoisted was soon wind-filled and taut, and the ships timbers felt again the sea-surge. Out over the waves the ship danced, rejoicing to feel again the foam at its throat. Like the warriors, that sea-boat longed to be home, rode the ocean, surf-skimmed the waves, until they saw at last the welcome cliffs and headlands of home, a coast they knew and loved. A favourable breeze brought them over the shallows and beached them safely on shore.

Their coming had not gone unnoticed from those homeland cliffs. Geatish coastguards had long been watching for their return, anxiously awaiting their beloved heroes. They were there on the beach helping to moor the boat, to hold it fast so that no sea-surge could harm this boat of heroes. They were there to help unload the heroes' golden hoard, marvelling at the amount of it, at the richness of it. They did not have far to carry it, for Hygelac, the Geatish king, lived with his war-band close by the sea wall itself.

News of their coming, of the hoard they carried, raced ahead of them to Hygelac himself, brave king of all the Geats. Beowulf, his nephew and greatest champion, his hearth-companion, had survived his perilous quest, and was returning home unscathed! By order of Hygelac the mead-hall was cleared at once and prepared for Beowulf and those honoured Geatish heroes. As he saw Beowulf and his warriors striding into the hall, Hygelac could scarcely contain his burning curiosity to hear all about their adventures in Denmark, and their miraculous return.

After all the greetings were done – there never was such a warmth of welcome – and the mead-cup had been offered around to each and every one of these heroes, the two noble kinsmen, Hygelac and Beowulf, sat down face to face, the one eager to know, the other eager to tell. Hygelac leaned forward, longing to hear.

"Tell us now, beloved brave Beowulf, how you survived this battle in distant Heorot. I warned you, did I not, of the dangers that lay ahead of you in Denmark. 'Do not go, dear friend,' I said, 'and face that murderous monster Grendel.' Those were my very words, if I remember. Yet you did not listen to my advice. You were determined to help Hrothgar, a friend in need, and I confess now I much admired you for it. Tell me now all that happened. Live it for us again, so we may know all you have done whilst you were gone."

So Beowulf told his story to his king – of how the Geats had been so royally welcomed to Heorot, that great mead hall, of Grendel's coming by night, how Handscio had been snatched up half asleep and ground to death in Grendel's jaws. "I grappled with this beast bare-handed, my lord Hygelac," said Beowulf, "grasped his arm and would not let him go. When he tore himself away, still I held his severed arm. Perhaps he thought he had escaped. But it was his death-wound, his life's blood draining out of him deep in his watery lair. So that monster died, and so I avenged all the hurt he had done to Hrothgar and the Danes. And generously that king rewarded me, just as he had promised, with a treasure-hoard of gold, rich and finely worked. And at Heorot all of us, Danish thanes and Geatish warriors, rejoiced. But we rejoiced too soon, for out of the night came Grendel's vengeful mother, a fiend filled with fury. She struck down the first she saw, Ashhere he was called, most beloved counsellor and dearest hearth-companion to Hrothgar, the old king. So I went after her. Seeking her lair, I plunged into the whirlpool of sea-serpents and found her there, this gruesome guardian of the deep. Hand to hand we fought. I was as near to death then as I have ever been. Saved only by God, and by a giant sword. With this I hewed off both their hideous heads, made an end to that family of monsters, slew the last of Satan's children, and brought peace again to Hrothgar and the Danish people. For all this the fair and generous king presented us with more treasures still, all of which, brave king, I have carried back for you, who are my only family."

Then Beowulf had them bring in all the treasures he had received from Hrothgar: a boar's head standard, helmet and war-shirt and sword, all of which had belonged to Hrothgar's own brother – no gift could have been more precious than all this garb of war, none more kindly meant. Four high-stepping horses were then led in, burnished bay they were and matching as apples. All these and more Beowulf gave that day to his lord. Surely there was never a more generous heart than this.

To Hygelac's queen he presented the marvellous ancient collar he had been given by Hrothgar, three prancing horses also and fine saddles too. Wearing this jewel the queen shone in beauty as never before. For all these great gifts, and to honour this great champion, Hygelac laid in Beowulf's lap the finest sword in the royal treasure. Richly wrought in gold it was, magnificent in every detail. But that was not all. The king bestowed on him there and then a huge estate and a fine hall too, fit for such a hero who had brought through his brave deeds such honour and such riches to the land of the Geats.

All seemed then peaceful and set fair for Hygelac and the Geats, but the fate of kings and their people, even of great heroes, is forever fickle and fraught with danger.

BEOWULF AND THE DEATH-DRAGON OF THE DEEP

It was not so many years after this that in the heat of battle, Hygelac, brave king of the Geats, was struck down and killed. He was much mourned for he had ruled wisely and well. But the Geats were fortunate indeed despite their sadness, for now the whole kingdom passed into the hands of that great hero, Beowulf. For over fifty years he ruled the land and ruled it fairly, generous always in spirit, a good and kindly king. Never had there been a king more loved and admired than Beowulf. Grey-haired now – even for this hero age had taken its toll of years – he had every right to expect a peaceful old age; but cruel fate was to intervene and deny it to him. We do not always have what we deserve.

For three hundred years or more, deep in a burial mound high on the cliffs above the moors, lay a hoard-guarding dragon, sleeping all this while undisturbed. So he might have stayed for ever, harmless in his dragon-dreams, a hoard of golden treasure for his bed. No one would ever have known of him, nor of the treasure. But quite by chance some nameless slave happened upon this cave. Condemned to a flogging and on the run from his warrior master, he found the opening, and seeking any shelter he could find, crept in and came across this slumbering dragon curled up on his pile of treasure; heaps of hoard-things there were.

Seized with sudden terror at the sight of this monstrous dragon the unfortunate slave wanted only to escape. But one golden goblet lay close by, so close he simply could not resist it. He snatched it up and ran for his life. And even as he ran an idea came into his head. This goblet would be a perfect gift for my master, he thought. I'll go back and give it to him. Maybe it will appease his fury. Little did he know what fire-fury he would bring upon himself and his whole people by this thoughtless act. Little did he know or care how this treasure came to be there with the death-dragon guarding it; how in a heathen age long ago one sole survivor from a whole tribe of earls, brought to a sudden and violent war-death, carried this treasure-hoard of talismans into the mound, for he knew he could no longer guard it and care for it himself. He decided to hide it, bury it where no one could ever find it. Over the treasure he bewailed his grief for his lost friends, for the joys they had shared, crying out to the earth itself to protect the precious tribe-treasure, last vestiges of a proud people now slaughtered and silent in death, all their harp playing, all singing, done for ever. So he left the treasure-filled mound, and maddened with grief wandered the wind-wild moors until death came for him too. So all that tribe was gone. But the treasure remained.

Soon there came that way a dreaded dragon, a night-ravager. A foul flame-fiend he was, always seeking out hellish hiding holes where he could rest. One day he happened on this same treasure-filled mound – fate had brought him there – and made it his own, possessed it with his power, sleeping there on this priceless pillow till the end of

time. Not that it did him any good. Possession was all his joy.
So for three hundred years undisturbed this death-dragon guarded
his underground hoard, until that doomed day when that wretched
slave came upon the place by chance, discovered the godless creature
sleeping there, and carried off that golden goblet, a peace-offering to
his master, so he thought. A luckless man. But the dragon through
his serpent scales had felt the loss of the treasure, and hearing the
footfall of the intruder, opened one angry eye and watched him go.
After three hundred years he was slow to wake. This worm of
wickedness now slithered out of his hole following where the
fleeing slave had gone. Rage-roaring he circled his mound looking

for the man's footprints, but found
none out there in the wilderness. Yet
he knew his treasure-house had been
breached, knew the golden cup had
been stolen from him and was burning
with fire-fury at the offence. He would
have his sweet revenge, that was sure. He longed now for the flames
of war, for the fire of battle again after so many years asleep. He
could hardly wait.

That night this death-dealing dragon came flying over the moors.
Armed with fire he came, spewing out his flames wherever he went.
He did not mind whose dwelling it was he left burning brightly
behind him. In his eyes all were guilty of the crime. If he had his
way he would not have left a single man alive. Over all the Geatish

land the blazing fires rose skyward. A scourge of fire-spitting destruction he wrought in that one night, pouring out his venomous fire, burning everywhere and everyone with his flame-throwing, poisonous breath. Before morning light came to the sky, with the country and its people left so cruelly ravaged, the serpent flew back to his hidden hoard deep inside his secret mound. Here he believed he would be quite safe. But he was mistaken, as you shall hear.

Beowulf had heard by now of the horror visited on his countrymen that night by this death-dragon. His own mead-hall, most magnificent of all buildings in the land, the very heart of his kingdom, had been consumed by the serpent's fire. Sorrow overcame him when he saw the ashes smouldering. Grief-gripped and guilt-ridden, that good king imagined he must have brought this on himself, that he had somehow angered his eternal God. When he saw how that devil's dragon had visited fire and fury on all the land by the sea, where his people had lived out their lives in peace, secure, they thought, in the safety of their homes, then anger swelled inside him and overcame his grief and his guilt. Now the old king roused himself to action and swore to punish this evil death-messenger.

Old he may have been, but Beowulf was formidable still in strength and will. At once he gave orders that a huge shield should be made, all in iron – he knew wood would be little use against the searing heat of the serpent's fire. Only with such a shield would he be able to come close enough to the hoard-squatting dragon to put an end to this murderer's miserable life. But Beowulf, this mighty warrior of old, would not go up against this death-dragon with his army of warriors. He was a hero who had never known fear. He scorned the dragon's strength and his fighting prowess too. Beowulf had survived battles in plenty and had emerged victorious in many other clashes since that time when he had destroyed the monster Grendel and his sea-hag mother all those years before in the land of Hrothgar. He was not afraid again to do battle in defence of his people, this noble hero. So he took only eleven warrior companions with him to seek out this fiery ravager of the night. They were all he would need, he thought.

But one more came with them too, the slave who had stumbled by chance into the hidden mound and woken the hoard-watching dragon from his centuries of sleep. He had been discovered, this guilty slave, been found clutching the precious golden goblet. So  the cause of the serpent's woeful attack had been discovered, and the slave was brought along, this cursed coward, to show them the way into the mound, for he alone knew the inside of the dragon's earth-hall, the cavernous lair heaped high with treasure, where the dreaded dragon lay. Beowulf knew how formidable this underground guardian was, how fierce and fiery a foe he would be. And he was not wrong.

To the headland on the cliffs they came and saw at last the secret mound and the narrow way in. Here Beowulf spoke to his trusted hearth-companions. He meant with his words to lift their hearts, to exhort and encourage them, to banish their fear. There was no fear in the great hero, but the truth was that his own spirit was gloomy and heavy with premonition, as if he already knew that this was the place and the time of his last fight, that this dragon would be the end of him, his body and soul torn apart at last in the struggle that lay ahead. Strongly he spoke though, banishing all those dark thoughts from his mind.

"Cherished comrades-in-arms, I have survived many struggles in my life and I do not forget any of them, nor the brave war-companions who died at my side. I have always had good fortune in these battles, wielding my bright, hard-edged sword again and again in service first of Hygelac, my king, in my early days, and as king myself now these long years since. Every battle I ventured I won, by God's good grace, and I shall win again today, old as I am. I am the stern guardian of my people and must destroy this death-dragon before he destroys us. I would go up against him bareheaded and bare-handed as I grappled once with that monster, Grendel. But I must somehow defend myself against the fire of this flame-spitter. So I will carry this iron shield to fend off the flames, and wear my mail-shirt and helmet to protect my flesh from his fire-venom. I shall be strong in spirit, give all in this fight. I shall not run from this heathen hoard-guardian, however hot and fierce his flames. Wait here for me. This is my fight. It is for me, your king, to match myself against this champion of evil. I will dare all bravely. Should I win, God willing, then the hoard-dragon will

die his death and harm us no more, and we shall win all the gold
he guards. Should I fail, then your king will not see this nightfall,
nor any other tomorrow, nor share the cup of mead with you ever
again. If this is my end, then so be it."

Strongly he spoke out, this champion of the Geats. Despite all his
doubts he was still confident in his prowess. Brave beside his
shield he stood, in helmet and war-shirt ready now to meet the
death-dragon face to face. He would not shrink from the fight,
this survivor of countless conflicts and battle-clashes. Then out of
the mound came a sudden blast of flame. Waves of savage fire
surged out of that deadly tunnel. So the dragon began the battle,
breathing out his perilous fire. Without being burnt alive there
seemed no way in, no way past those terrible flames for Beowulf.

In his anger now the hero roared his defiance. Like a battle-horn
it sounded, echoing through the vaulted cavern. Deep inside,
the hated dragon recognized the champion's voice-challenge.
Filled with fury he stirred himself to violent action. Uncoiled
now the serpent roared out his thunderous response, a hissing
gout of foul flame and billowing breath-smoke. The ground
shook. The rocks and the trees trembled as the death-dragon
emerged enraged from the mound, seeking out his foe. There

 stood Beowulf before him,
bravest of warrior kings,
his shield held before him,
his trusted sword drawn.

Each saw then the terrible power of the other, felt the same portent of impending doom. But neither would shirk the death-encounter. Beowulf stood his ground as the all-enveloping flames rushed forward towards him, curling over and around him, enveloping him entirely in smoke and fire.

76

Bravely he stood fast behind his great shield, knowing already that, huge though it was, it was too small to protect him. Undaunted the hero swung up his huge ancestral sword, ancient sword of all the Geatish kings, and struck the dragon a savage, scything blow, cut through his foul flesh to the bare bone beneath, a deathblow he meant it to be, hoped it would be. But this time his good old sword failed to bite deeply enough. Wounded now the dragon came on in his agony, spat his hellish fire over the great-hearted king, forced him back with his spewing flames. Beowulf felt the skin-searing pain and knew then that this time there would be no easy victory, that he had met his match at last.

Then as the death-dragon raged and roared, rearing up to attack Beowulf again, those chosen few, those trusted comrades-in-arms who should have rushed to his side in his moment of need, turned away and ran for the safety of the woods, saving their shameful skins, leaving their king to face that flame-belching monster all alone. Only Wiglaf the youngest there, stood by his lord. He felt the bonds of kinship more keenly than the others. He knew his duty, knew where his place was. He would not desert the king who had bestowed on him and his family so much kindness. Land he held and a wealthy house and gold too, all given to him and his forebears by this most generous of all kings. He would stay and fight at Beowulf's side. Angrily he urged the others to do the same, shouting after them: "How can you leave him now, when he needs us most, our dear lord Beowulf? Did he not choose us himself to accompany him on this perilous adventure? Did we not all come here expecting a fight? Now when we should be at his side, you run away like rabbits! As for me I would far rather die here alongside him, feel with him the pain of death if I must, end my life fighting in the struggle, sword in hand, rather that than desert him and return home shamed for ever."

But his words fell on deaf ears. Fear-filled, the cowards dropped their swords and ran for their lives, all courage withered suddenly and gone, and all honour with it.

Wiglaf did not hesitate now. Disdaining all fear – and this was his first battle – the young lion threw up his wooden shield and strode through the battle-smoke to his lord's side. "Beloved and best Beowulf, I am here to help you. I shall defend you to the death, my king, as I have sworn to do." Just as he spoke the death-dragon attacked for a second time, seeking out both hated foe-men with his blast of flame. In that billow of fire the youngster's shield was at once burnt, reduced to cinders, and his mail-shirt was melted away in the heat as if it had simply never been there. So the young kinsman leapt in behind the old king's shield. New strength surged into Beowulf's heart as he saw now that he was not alone in his fight any more. He sprang up once again from behind his shield and struck at the fire-snorting snake with all his might. But his iron blade snapped. That ancient sword of sternest steel, which had never before failed him in battle, failed him now and left him at the mercy of the pitiless monster who came down upon him now for the third time.

Now was the demon-dragon's chance, and he took it. Seething with war-hatred he opened his bitter jaws and seized the champion by the neck. The serpent's fangs bit deep into the flesh, and Beowulf's lifeblood poured from him. Wiglaf, that young hero, was as good as his word. His courage did not fail him now. He summoned all his strength and sprang forward into the dragon's fire to defend his lord. Hands and head were burnt as he came through it, but he was not to be put off, this brave warrior.

80

He would do his duty. Wiglaf did not aim for the scaly head of the beast, but went instead for the soft throat, stabbing deep into it with his sword, a thrust so powerful that the dragon was forced to loosen his grip on Beowulf, so stunning that the fiery flow was suddenly stemmed and staunched for ever. Coming again to his senses the great king seized his moment, whipped out his battle-sharp dagger, and drove it to the hilt into the dragon's body. So together the two heroes downed the dragon. They did not stop stabbing him till an  end was made of him, till his last gasp of life, the last death-breath, was over and the monster was still.

But for Beowulf this was to be his last victory of so many, and he knew it already. The poison in his wounds was beginning to burn and swell inside him. He sat down heavily on a ledge of rock, knowing the shadow of his own death was upon him, feeling the fatal pain of it boiling in his chest. Wiglaf, ever attentive to his lord and friend, ever loyal, bathed his bloodied king, unfastened his helmet, did all he could to staunch the bleeding, to relieve his pain. But death he could not staunch. No one can. The fearless leader knew well now that this was the end of his time, of all his earthly happiness.

He had only one wish to fulfil before his life left him. He called Wiglaf closer, for his speech was thin now, his breathing short. "Go now, dear friend," he said. "Go into the mound and find this dead serpent's treasure-hoard. I want to see it with my own eyes before I die, those ancient jewels, your golden inheritance. Just once I want to see it."

Wiglaf did not hesitate to obey his lord. Bloodied and burnt as he was, he ran past the dead hoard-guardian and into the barrow, deep into that house of treasures, into the winged serpent's den of darkness. Many and magnificent were the marvels he found there: old tarnished relics of a vanished ancient race of warriors, piles of drinking cups and heaps of helmets and twisted torcs, all of the most precious gold. No wonder this death-dragon had fought so hard to keep it. And high above the hoard there hung the battle-standard of the tribe, woven entirely in glowing gold that shone even in the gloom of the place, brightly enough even to light up the treasure below. Swiftly, for he knew there was little time to waste, Wiglaf gathered all he could carry out, golden cups and flagons, and that ancient battle-standard too.

Even burdened by his load of treasures Wiglaf ran all the way back out of the tunnel. With every eager step he worried that his lord might already have died out there while he was gone. And when the brave thane at last saw his leader he did seem almost dead, barely breathing still, his eyes closed. Wiglaf sprinkled his face with cooling water, begging him to wake up and live.

Deep in his death-sleep the battle-king heard Wiglaf's voice calling him back, opened his eyes and saw the gold honest Wiglaf had brought to show him. He thanked the youngster for all he had done for him – he was thoughtful even in death this hero – and then, breathless, spoke these last few words. "I have defended my kingdom these fifty years as best I could, served my people as wisely as I could. For that I thank my God, the King of all Glory. And to Him also I give thanks for these treasures I see before my dying eyes, for the opportunity to acquire them for my people on my death-day, to sustain them in all their needs in the future when I am gone. Wiglaf, my beloved friend, I fear I can stay no longer. Tell them – and this is the last command of their king – to build me a tomb high on the cliff overlooking Hronesness. Let it stand always as a towering reminder of me to my people, so that masted ships dipping through the sea-mists may see it and remember it always. Let the place be known for ever as Beowulf's barrow."

So saying he unclasped the golden collar from around his neck and gave it to Wiglaf. His helmet, armour and arm-rings too he handed to the young spearman, reward for his courage and loyalty. "Use these well, good friend," he said. These were the old man's last words, spoken with his last breath. At that moment his soul left his body, soaring heavenwards on its way to everlasting glory.

How Wiglaf grieved then at the passing of his king, at the suffering of his life's end.

It was no consolation to him that nearby lay the corpse of the terrible death-dragon, no joy to him that the destroyer had been destroyed, that he would no longer fly the night air, no longer terrorize and torment the people. It was no matter either that the beautiful treasure-hoard of unimaginable wealth was theirs.

Not long afterwards those ten traitorous battle-shirkers, those cringing cowards who had deserted their leader so shamefully decided it was safe enough to emerge from the woods. They came now to where the old king lay, and found Wiglaf, weary with battle, weeping at his lord's shoulder, still trying to wake him with water, still not wanting to believe the hero would not wake from his death-sleep, would never speak again. But as stillness gripped the old man's body, he saw and understood there was no life left, nor any hope of life either.

He turned his gaze then and his anger on those craven companions-in-arms gathered around. "Look well upon this lord of men, who made you who you are, gave you all you have and hold. But all his kindnesses to you were wasted, were they not? For when he most needed you, you turned and ran away. He had to face the fire-fury of this death-dragon alone and unaided. I could do little for him on my own, though I tried my best. All the world shall now hear how you deserted your lord and kinsman, turned tail and fled with never a thought for your king in his hour of greatest need. You thought only of your own worthless skins. For this shameful act you will pay a heavy price, I promise you. You will be stripped of all riches and honours, all possessions, even your homes. You and yours will be condemned to wander the world as beasts, homeless and friendless for ever."

News of the great king's death spread fast, how he had tried all he could to kill the death-dragon, and had indeed achieved it at last, but at a terrible cost. Both lay dead now on their slaughter-bed by the mound, Wiglaf, the young spearman, the only one who had stood by him in the fight, still at his master's side. On hearing these hateful tidings the earls in the royal mead-hall, saddened and silent, sat by their shields, fearful now for the safety of their kingdom, for the lord of the Geats, so long their strong protector, so long their guardian against every enemy, was gone from them for ever. Still unwilling and unable to believe this dread news, the war-band went heavy-hearted and with welling tears to where Beowulf lay. And so they saw the body for themselves, and knew then that the final day had come for their champion, that the warrior-king of the Geats was indeed dead.

They saw too that loathsome dragon stretched out nearby, scorched by his own flames, twisted and coiled in his death-agony. Over fifty foot long he was, this vile creature, once master of darkness, once their terrible tormentor, now laid low and destroyed by brave Beowulf. And they found there too all the treasure-hoard the death-dragon had been guarding. At Wiglaf's command, they fetched all of it out from inside the mound, bowls and flagons and platters, all in gold, wonderfully worked weapons too, arm-rings and jewels hidden for a thousand years from human eye until this moment. Neither they, as they gazed in awe at this precious pile, nor indeed Beowulf himself, could ever have known that the sole survivor of the earls who so long ago had placed the treasure for safe-keeping there had laid a curse on it to last till the end of time, that whoever found it and plundered it would bring down upon himself and his people nothing but terror and tragedy. And so it had happened.

Wiglaf lifted his head and spoke to these grief-stricken earls. "Before he died, our dear king asked me to present to you his last orders. We are to raise on the place of the funeral pyre, high on the hill at Hronesness, a barrow so that his name should never be forgotten. It shall be known always as Beowulf's barrow. And I say it must be the most magnificent, the most imposing barrow ever built, a place fitting for this most honoured and honourable of all warrior war-kings that ever lived. But first let us dispose of the remains of this fiend of hell, this death-dragon who has brought us so much suffering. The very sight of him offends my eye and sickens my heart." So they pushed the death-dragon over the edge of the cliff and watched as his body fell on the rocks below and broke there. The sea took him and covered him.

Then the earls made a bier and carried their beloved king to the hill at Hronesness. Firewood was brought from far and wide to build the funeral pyre. All around it they hung shining war-coats, battle-shields and helmets, as befitting the great hero they had lost. On the very top they laid him out, just as he had ordered. Wiglaf it was who set the torch to the pyre, kindled the biggest funeral pyre ever seen. Wind-fanned, the flames roared up through the pyre and consumed their cherished lord.

As the cloud of black smoke drifted high over the ocean, there could be heard the wailing and weeping of the women, the warriors and all his people, a song of sorrow that rose with the billowing smoke. Heaven swallowed both.

Then just as Beowulf had commanded, the Geats built for their dead leader a beacon on that headland, so high and huge that all seafarers could see it for miles around. Deep in his tomb they laid the ashes that remained from the fire, and placed there too all the jewels and torcs, all that magnificent treasure-hoard they had recovered from the dragon's mound. They left it there in the earth's keeping. And there it is to this day, no more use to men than ever it was before. Then the warriors rode round and round this walled barrow, last resting place of their hero king, and mourned him, told out loud their grief in lavish words praising his name and his prowess, honouring him as their lord and friend. Of all the kings that ever lived, they said, this was the gentlest and kindest to his people, the most gracious and famous the world had known. His life might be over, they said, but his name and his deeds would live on as long as his tale was told.

which is why, all these years Later, i have told this tale.